D1381558

To Matthew

Text and illustrations copyright © 1980 by Jenny Partridge
Published by World's Work Ltd
The Windmill Press, Kingswood, Tadworth, Surrey
Layout and design by The Romany Studio Workshop
Reproduced by Graphic Affairs Ltd, Southend
Printed in Great Britain by
William Clowes (Beccles) Limited, Beccles and London
SBN 437 66173 3

Peterkin Pollensnuff

JENNY PARTRIDGE

A WORLD'S WORK CHILDREN'S BOOK

Peterkin Pollensnuff whistled loudly
as he rode his bicycle along the riverbank.
"I'm so hungry," he thought. "Maybe,
if I hurried, I could finish
my paper-round and be back home

in time for another breakfast."
He pedalled round a corner at great speed,
and then suddenly swerved
to avoid a huge snail
that was lazily crossing the path!

The bicycle skidded, and crashed into a prickly bramble bush. Peterkin fell off, scattering newspapers everywhere.

"Creeping caterpillars!" he gasped, rubbing his head. The snail merely frowned at him and carried on.

Peterkin pulled his bicycle
from the brambles and saw,
with a sinking heart,
that the front tyre had a puncture!

"Oh no," he cried. "However can I do
my paper-round now?"
A large and colourful dragonfly brushed
past him. "Hallo, young wood mouse,"
she said, landing on a twig. "Why are
you so sad on such a fine day?"

"Oh, Dorelia, my bicycle has
a puncture," muttered Peterkin,
"and I simply must deliver these
newspapers before school."
He sniffed and swallowed hard.

"Hush now, there's no need to cry,"
said the dragonfly.
"I'm not crying," snapped Peterkin.

"I've – I've got a cold, that's all."
"Well, if you cheer up and wipe your eyes,
I shall do your paper-round for you,"
the dragonfly offered.
Peterkin blew his nose loudly.

"Gosh," he giggled, feeling much better.
"Won't everyone be surprised when
a dragonfly delivers their papers!"
"Hmm, maybe," said Dorelia, preening
her wings. "It would certainly help folks
to realise just how useful dragonflies can
be. Now, where do you want me to go?"

Peterkin gathered up his papers
and put the bag on her back.
"Mayfly Manor first please," he said.
"And then Mr Squint the mole, and last of all
the Twitchers at Clover Cottage.
You won't get lost, will you?"

"Get lost?" exclaimed the indignant
dragonfly, "I shall be back
before you can say 'Creeping caterpillars'!"
Tossing her gossamer wings,
she flew off with the bag of newspapers
streaming out behind her. Happily,
Peterkin began to mend his bicycle.

Dorelia zoomed up the pathway
of Mayfly Manor, just as old Colonel Grunt
set out for his morning stroll.
"Good heavens!" he said, astonished,
as his newspaper landed on the ground.

He looked up and could hardly believe
his eyes. His morning paper
being delivered by a dragonfly?
He must be imagining things.
"Too much elderberry port, old chap,"
he told himself.

The dragonfly flew on
and arrived at Mr Squint's house,
where the old mole
was busily polishing his windows.

A newspaper dropped out of the sky
and hit him on the nose. "Good morning
Mr Squint!" called Dorelia.
"Well bless my soul!" he cried,
adjusting his glasses.

On she flew, over Harebell Heath
until she saw old Grandpa Twitcher
in his garden. "Grandma, quick!"
he called, as his morning paper
floated down towards him.

He hobbled down the path,
pointing up at the dragonfly.
Not looking where he was going,
his foot caught in a tangle of ivy,
and over he toppled!

"What *is* going on?"
called Grandma Twitcher.
"Up there," shouted Grandpa excitedly.
"Look! A dragonfly delivering the papers!"
But by then, Dorelia had flown away,
and the sky was empty.

"Nonsense, whoever heard of such a thing.
You're getting as silly as a snail,"
scolded Grandma Twitcher,
helping him to his feet.
"Come along and I'll make you
a nice cup of blackberry leaf tea."

The paper-round finished,
the dragonfly flew back over Bilberry Hill
and landed beside Peterkin.

"Goodness," she said as he helped her
to take off the newspaper bag.
"That was heavy."

"Thank you, I really don't know
what I would have done without you,"
said Peterkin gratefully.

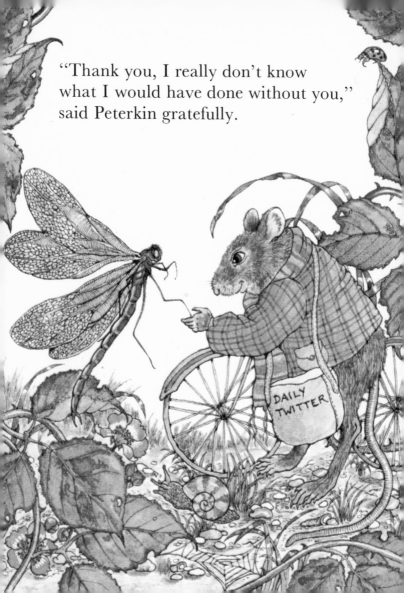

"It was lucky I was passing,"
she remarked, "but now I must go.
I have a thousand and one things
to do today.
Look after that cold of yours!"

The wood mouse smiled,
and watched her fly over the tall grass,
her wings glistening in the morning sun.

"I might have time for another
breakfast after all," he thought,
and he pedalled swiftly
along the riverbank towards home.